Four Fierce Kittens

Joyce Dunbar
Pictures by Jakki Wood

SCHOLASTIC
HARDCOVER

SCHOLASTIC INC. · New York

For Joanna
J.D.

For Rebecca Neal   Molly Martin
Alexandra Burkart
J.W.

Library of Congress Cataloging-in-Publication Data

Dunbar, Joyce.
    Four fierce kittens / by Joyce Dunbar ; pictures by Jakki Wood.
        p.   cm.
    Summary: Four little kittens in search of excitement try to frighten the
barnyard animals, with no effect, until they meet a friendly puppy.
    ISBN 0-590-45535-4
    [1. Cats—Fiction.   2. Domestic animals—Fiction.]   I. Wood.
Jakki, ill.   II. Title.
PZ7.D8944Fo   1991
[E]—dc20   91-26939
                                                               CIP
                                                               AC

12 11 10 9 8 7 6 5 4 3 2 1   2 3 4 5 6 7/9

Printed in Belgium

First Scholastic printing, May 1992

Fat mother cat was asleep on her mat.

Said her four little kittens,
"There's no fun in that!"
And off they went to run wild
on the farm.

Said the marmalade kitten, spiking his claws,
"I am a terrible tiger!
I will hunt the hen out of her hutch!"

And he tried to growl,
but he didn't know how.
He could only go . . .

meow   meow

And the hen went

CLUCK   CLUCK   CLUCK

"I didn't know she could do that!"
said the marmalade kitten, and he jumped away.

Said the black little kitten,
with a glint in her eye,
"I am a panther on the prowl.
I will frighten the pig out of his sty."

And she tried to howl,
but she didn't know how.
She could only go . . .

meow   meow

And the pig went

OINK

OINK

OINK

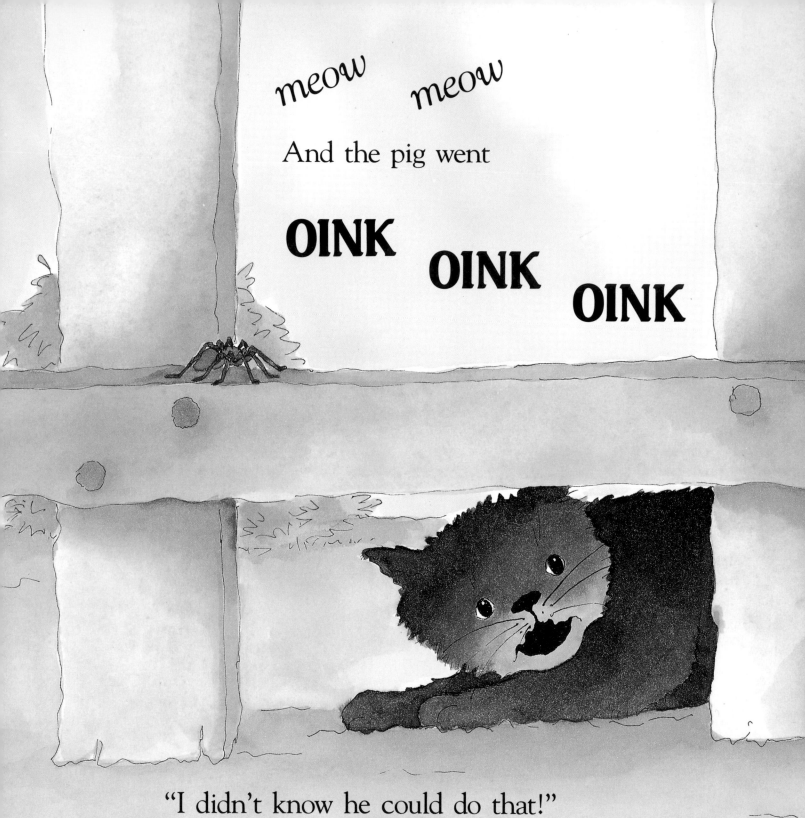

"I didn't know he could do that!"
said the black little kitten, and she slinked away.

Said the tortoiseshell kitten,
pricking his ears,
"I am a leaping leopard!
I will chase the duck into her pond!"

And he tried to snarl,
but he didn't know how.
He could only go . . .

meow   meow

And the duck went

QUACK   QUACK

QUACK

"I didn't know she could do that!"
said the tortoiseshell kitten, and he leapt away.

Said the tabby little kitten, twitching her tail,
"I am a dangerous lion!
I will make the sheep run down the lane."

And she tried to roar,
but she didn't know how.
She could only go . . .

And the sheep went

BAA

BAA BAA

"I didn't know they could do that!"
said the tabby little kitten,
and she sprang away.

Said the four little kittens, ever so fierce,
"We are tigers! Panthers! Leopards! Lions!
We will scare that gaggle of geese!"

And they tried to roar,
to snarl, to growl,
and they managed to go . . .

meow-l   meow-l

But the geese went

HONK

HONK

HONK

"We didn't know they could do that!"
The four fierce kittens tumbled away.

Then a puppy came over to play.
And the puppy went . . .

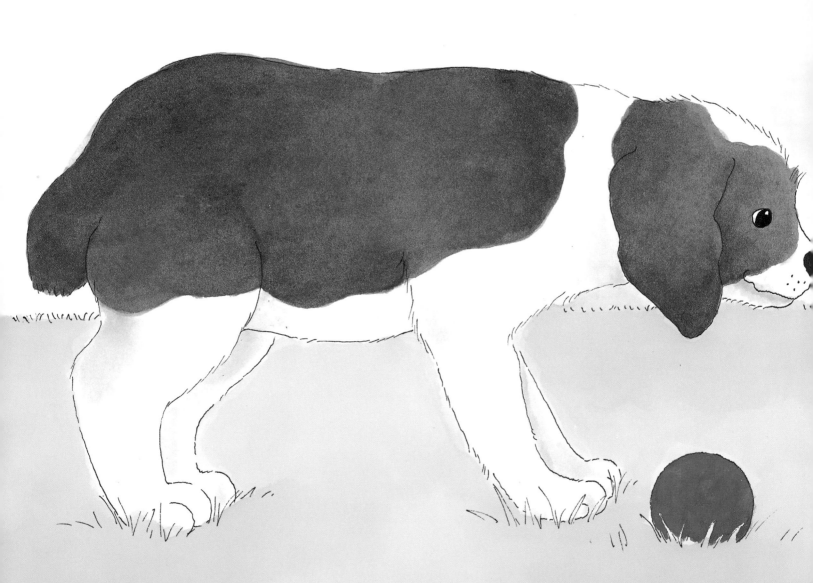

BOW WOW WOW

Then those four fierce kittens
arched their backs.
Their fur stood on end.
They hissed. They spat!

And that terrified puppy
ran away . . .

SCAT

Said those proud little kittens,
"We didn't know we could do THAT!"

And they went back to their mother
to sleep on the mat.